Mo
and J_____'s
Big Break

Mumbo
and Jumbo's
Big Break

Written and Illustrated by
DON CONROY

POOLBEG
FOR CHILDREN

Published 2001
by Poolbeg Press Ltd
123 Baldoyle Industrial Estate
Dublin 13, Ireland
E-mail: poolbeg@poolbeg.com
www.poolbeg.com

1 3 5 7 9 10 8 6 4 2

A catalogue record for this book is available from the British Library.

ISBN 1 84223 083 2

Cover design by Steven Hope
Illustrations by Don Conroy
Typeset by Patricia Hope in Times 16/24
Printed by The Guernsey Press Ltd,
Vale, Guernsey, Channel Islands.

About the Author

Don Conroy is Ireland's best-loved illustrator and writer for children. He is also a television personality and an enthusiastic observer of wildlife.

Also by Don Conroy

Wildlife Colouring Book
The Fox's Tale
What The Owl Saw
The Vampire Journal
The Anaconda from Drumcondra
The Elephant At The Door
The Bookworm Who Turned Over A New Leaf
Rocky The Dinosaur
Seal Of Approval
Cartoon Crazy

For Sarah

"Wake up, sleepybones," squawked Doris the ostrich. "It's nearly midday and the concert is starting soon." Jumbo the hippo blinked open his big eyes.

"Who? What? Where? Oh, it's you, Doris," he yawned. "You gave me quite a start. I was having this beautiful dream – it was about . . ."

"You can't be late for the concert," snapped Doris. "The king, queen and the pride will be in attendance. I'm sure the entire jungle folk will be there as well."

"Just give me forty winks more," yawned Jumbo, "so I can finish my lovely dream." The hippo slipped below the water down onto the riverbed and snuggled up in the soft mud.

"Jumbo, Jumbo," Doris yelled. "Oh, he's impossible!" She stared at her reflection in the water. "Look at me," she said. "I couldn't sleep all night with excitement at the thought of the annual concert. Of course, having to organise it all by myself is no easy task."

"What's up?" asked Crackle the croc who was basking on the riverbank.

"Oh, good day, Crackle! I was just explaining . . ."

"To yourself?" said Crackle as he looked at her mirror image in the water. "I'd be careful of that," he grinned. "Some folks might think that talking to oneself is very strange."

Doris ruffled her feathers. "Listen, Crackle . . ."

"It's OK – I don't think you're odd or strange."

"What do you mean?" she snapped at him.

"No need to snap at me," he retorted. "Besides," he chuckled, "I'm the biggest snapper around these parts. You get it?" He winked and nudged her.

"Oh dear," said Doris, "there are mornings like this when I just want to bury my head in the sand."

"Listen, Doris, if you need someone to talk to, just call on me. Of course, make sure I'm well fed at the time." He grinned. "Just kidding."

"Listen, buster, if you can't be of help just clear off," said Doris.

A tear came out of the crocodile's eye. "A guy would need to be thick-skinned around these parts with some of the abuse I have to put up with." He began to waddle away.

"Oh, I'm sorry! I didn't mean to snap at you," called Doris.

Crackle grinned. "These crocodile tears work every time. How about a date?"

"Will you please be serious for a moment and listen?"

"I'm all ears," said Crackle.

"The concert is happening today near the watering hole," explained Doris.

"I'll be there," said Crackle.

"There will be no show if Jumbo doesn't show up."

"I get it," said Crackle. "You weren't talking to yourself at all but to Jumbo who is at the bottom of the river."

"The penny has dropped," said Doris.

"Leave it to me," said Crackle and he slipped quietly into the water, then disappeared below. Doris watched and waited.

Crackle spied Jumbo lolling about.

"I know how to shift him," Crackle smirked. He sneaked up on Jumbo, opened his jaws and snapped them down on his bottom. Jumbo gave a shriek.

Doris watched as the water seemed to boil, then Jumbo tore out of the water at great speed and straight into a tree.

"Ouch," he yelled.

"Oh dear," said Doris, "are you all right?"

"I think so," Jumbo grumbled. "You were right! I should never have gone back to sleep – because my lovely dream turned into a nightmare."

"I wonder why?" smiled Doris, looking at Crackle who just popped up. He gave her a wink and chuckled. Jumbo went over to the waterfall and washed off all the mud.

"Ooh, aah," he shivered, "that's better. Very refreshing. Well, Doris, I'm all set. Let's go. My audience awaits me."

Off they set for the waterhole, Doris leading the way, followed by Jumbo and Crackle. Jumbo could be heard before he was seen because he was practising and exercising his voice. His big booming voice echoed around the jungle. By the time they arrived a large crowd had already gathered. Zebras, wildebeest, gazelles, elands and waterhogs sat one side. Leopards, cheetahs, servals, lions, crocodiles, elephants, rhinos, hippos, gorillas and baboons sat on the other.

The giraffes didn't mind sitting at the back – no matter where they sat they always had a good view on account of their long necks. The monkeys, birds and snakes all sat in the trees. There wasn't a branch that wasn't occupied, from the giant harpy eagle to the weaver bird. The smaller animals like the weasels, meercats, badgers, foxes, jackals, armadillos, porcupines and mongooses all sat up front with the frogs, toads, shrews, mice and rats. Even the bats were awake. They didn't want to miss this exciting show.

Mumbo the elephant was walking up and down, anxiously awaiting the arrival of Jumbo. Nobody could see how nervous she was because she was behind a large curtain made of branches and banana leaves, constructed for her by the mountain gorillas. She would have to perform on her own if he didn't show up. As most of their songs were

duets this made things rather awkward.
Still, she had a large repertoire of songs
and if she had to sing on her own she
would, especially with royalty present.
Luckily that wasn't to be, for Jumbo
arrived just in the nick of time and sneaked
behind the curtain.

"About time," she scolded him. "Everyone is here."

"Relax, dear Mumbo! The pride haven't arrived yet and we're the final act."

"I guess you're right." She took some water up in her trunk and put it into her mouth, then began to gargle.

"They're here," squawked Doris as she peeped behind the curtain. Mumbo got so nervous that she shot the water out all over Doris.

"Oh, I'm most dreadfully sorry," said Mumbo, looking at a very wet ostrich.

"Never mind," sighed Doris. "My feathers are drip-dry."

Then Goo Goo the silver-backed gorilla walked out in front of the crowd.

"Salutations, one and all! Will you all put your claws, hooves or wings together and welcome the royal family!"

The crowds began to cheer, shriek, clap and some even banged heads together in excitement. The pride moved in very regally and took up the best position.

The gorilla banged on his chest. "Pray silence for His Royal Majesty."

Real the lion stepped forward and brushed back his mane.

"Dear subjects, the queen and the family are so looking forward to the concert."

The king and queen took their seats and everyone else sat down and relaxed.

The gorilla cleared his throat.

"Well, we have an exciting line-up this afternoon, starting with Chinwag the chimp." There was a big cheer as the chimpanzee bounded up onto the stage.

Chinwag began his act by pulling faces and mimicking other animals, especially Goo Goo the gorilla. The crowd loved it. He pulled himself upright.

"Did you hear the one about the chimp who used to swing about in the trees with a banana in each ear? Well, one day he was stopped by a baboon who said to him, 'Excuse me, you have bananas in your ears!' 'What?' said the chimp. The baboon repeated, 'You have bananas in your ears!' 'Sorry, I can't hear you,' said the chimp. 'I've got bananas in my ears.'." The crowd hooted with laughter. Chinwag was great at warming up an audience.

After that, Pit the rock python slithered on stage.

"Will you please give a warm welcome to Pit the rock python and she doesn't mind if you hiss," the gorilla quipped.

The python began to move to strange jungle rhythms played by the monkeys on drums and a stringed instrument. Pit could reach to a height as tall as the giraffe then would turn her body into amazing shapes before returning to the ground in a most graceful way.

"Enchanting," yelled the lioness. The king nodded in agreement and smiled broadly. The show continued with a great variety of acts. Surprisingly smoothly, thought Doris the ostrich – still she kept her toes crossed just in case. Alpha the old baboon told amazing stories about his home in the Mountains of the Dragons. Large flocks of songbirds sang beautiful dawn-chorus melodies.

"What an exciting show we've had so far," beamed Goo Goo. "Well, now we come to the part of the show you've all been waiting for. Please give a good jungle welcome to

Mumbo the elephant and Jumbo the hippo."
There were loud roars, hooves stomping and
wings clapping, from the crowds.

"You're on," said Doris anxiously.

Jumbo whispered, "I can't go on. I've lost
my voice." When Doris heard this she passed
out. Jumbo looked down at Doris who was in
a dead faint. "Oops," he smiled awkwardly
to Mumbo. "I was just kiddin'."

"Come on," snapped Mumbo and pushed
him out on stage.

The gorilla stretched his arm out.

"I hardly need to introduce the finest
singers on the African continent but would
you please welcome Mumbo and Jumbo!"

The crowd went wild. Mumbo and
Jumbo bowed towards the king and queen.

"Your Royal Highnesses," said Mumbo
coyly, "we are honoured to sing for you.
Isn't that right, Jumbo?"

"Oh yeah," said the hippo, "sure thing." Mumbo nudged Jumbo. "I mean Your Kingship and Worship," Jumbo blurted. "We will begin with the duet from *The Pearl Fishers* by Bizet."

"Oh, this is my favourite," said the queen. You could hear a pin drop as the elephant and the hippo sang the beautiful aria.

What the animals didn't know was that while they were enjoying the concert a large group of men were making their way through the jungle with one thing on their minds - to capture as many animals as possible. Their plan was to sell them all to the zoos in Europe or America, depending on who would pay the most money. As they made their way through the dense jungle they heard the most beautiful singing. They had no idea where it was coming from. They could only assume that one of the local natives had got hold of a gramophone or victrolla somewhere and was playing records.

Snide Ramsbottom, the leader of the expedition, ordered one of the native carriers to climb a tree to see if he could see who was playing the music. The native quickly climbed a boboa tree. Ramsbottom turned to his assistant leader Fred Fortune.

"Something very peculiar is going on here. We've trekked through this jungle for two hours and we haven't heard one bird or seen one animal."

"Too true," said Fortune. "Something fishy is going on."

"Hey, boss," yelled the man in the tree, "I see an amazing sight, most amazing, boss, absolutely amazing!"

"Would you mind sharing this amazing sight with us," snapped Ramsbottom.

"Animals and birds everywhere," shouted the man. "In the clearing at the waterhole." "So that's it," smirked Ramsbottom. "They're all drinking at the waterhole. No wonder we didn't see any."

He ordered his men to set up traps everywhere. Nets, pits, and traps were placed all around different parts of the jungle. The men worked quickly digging pits, placing nets on trees, disguising cages by covering them with foliage.

"You did well, men," said Ramsbottom when they had finished. "And if we play our cards right we can be on the steamboat by the end of the week heading back home with animals worth their weight in gold."

The men laughed loudly and patted each other on the back.

"A bonus to every man who fills those crates and cages," said Ramsbottom. "For now, we'll just sit and wait." He still couldn't figure out where all the beautiful singing was coming from.

That evening the concert finished to great applause. Flowers were showered on Mumbo and Jumbo. The king thanked everyone for a most enjoyable show and was generous in his praise of Doris the ostrich for organising the event. "It even

topped last year's which seemed an impossible task," he added. Doris blushed and bowed gracefully with wings displayed.

"Excellent show," hooted the eagle owl.

There was more applause. The sun began to dip low in the sky as the animals and other creatures began to make their way home. They had no idea what lay in store for them behind the dense vegetation. The

rhino stopped in his tracks and began to sniff the air. He thought he could get the scent of humans.

"Move along," said another rhino.

Next minute the animals and wildfolk were thrown into total panic. Some had fallen into pits; others had walked into net traps. There were loud shrieks and alarm calls as they rushed to escape the terrible traps. But the men were too clever and expert at capturing wild animals. Animal after animal was trapped, even the birds didn't escape the cannon nets that were shot into the air bringing down eagles, hawks, storks, owls and many a sunbird. In all the excitement and panic animals ran into each other, accidentally knocking each other into the deep pits. Snakes slithered into black holes for cover only to discover they were tube traps.

"Oh dear, this is a disaster," wailed Doris as she watched the king and queen having a net sprung over them. The men rushed over to secure the pride with spiked poles and ropes.

"What's up?" asked Jumbo who just came on the scene with Mumbo.

"What's up?" she shrieked. "The entire jungle folk are in trouble, that's what's up!"

"What should we do?" asked Jumbo.

"Well, I'm not usually a violent bird but I'm going to make an exception today." She ran over and gave one of the men a kick in the bottom and another a kick in the stomach. "Take that!" she squawked.

"Good on you!" yelled Mumbo.

"You show them," said Jumbo.

Well, Doris distracted the men so much that the pride managed to slip out from under the large net and escape to safety.

Doris was very pleased to see the pride get away. Next minute two men jumped on Doris and forced her to the ground, quickly tying her up.

"That's not fair!" yelled Mumbo.

"There's nothing for it but to charge them," said Jumbo. The elephant and the hippo stamped their feet. "On the count of three we'll charge," said Jumbo. Mumbo nodded. "One, two, three, charge!" yelled Jumbo. They rushed at the men who quickly got out of their way. Mumbo and Jumbo charged through the undergrowth, the elephant just ahead of the hippo.

Mumbo only just managed to stop herself from falling into a deep pit full of antelopes and rhinos. "Oops, that was a near thing," she sighed in relief.

But Jumbo couldn't stop himself in time and crashed into Mumbo sending her into the pit. Luckily for the animals below they managed to get out of the way just in time, narrowly escaping Mumbo's large frame falling on them.

"Oops, very sorry," said Jumbo. "I'll get some help." He didn't realise a man had sneaked up behind him until he prodded him in the bottom with a spiked pole. "Ouch," yelled Jumbo as he leaped into the air. "Watch out below," he shouted as he fell into the pit, landing on top of Mumbo.

"Aaaaah!" she shrieked. "You nearly flattened me."

"Thanks for breaking my fall, dear Mumbo."

"Don't mention it," groaned Mumbo. "Just get off."

"What will we do?" asked a gazelle.

"Well, we mustn't panic," said Jumbo. Then he began to panic and tried in vain to climb up the clay walls. "We're doomed. Help!" he shrieked. "They're going to eat us."

"Stay calm," said Mumbo. "Nobody is going to eat you. They have other plans for us, I don't know what, but we're safe for the moment."

"Speaking of eating," said Jumbo, "do

you smell something cooking, like sausages? It sure smells good."

"What's up with you?" snapped Mumbo. "You're a vegetarian."

"Oh yes, you're right. I forgot."

Mumbo shook her head.

"They will feed us?" said the hippo. "They'll hardly let us starve?"

"How can you think of food at a time like this?" snapped a rhino.

"Easy," said Jumbo. "I think of food nearly all the time."

The men were pleased with their work. In fact, they couldn't believe how lucky they were in catching such a variety of animals all together. Many creatures escaped but they didn't mind. They felt they had captured the most important ones, like leopards, cheetahs, lions, giraffes, zebras, rhinos and several varieties of antelope. They had only managed to capture one elephant and one hippo. They also had a fine collection of birds which would fetch a good price. Darkness fell. The animals could hear the men making merry. The animals were all silent and sombre. Some felt very lonely. They didn't know what the future would hold or where they would be taken. The stars and the moon looked down on them.

"What a way for such a lovely day to end," sobbed Mumbo.

Early next morning the animals were loaded into crates and cages. Some put up a fight but there were just too many men with ropes and nets. The rest went quietly into the cages. Mumbo was grateful she was put into the same cage as Jumbo.

The leader, Ramsbottom, inspected his prize cargo. He stared in at Mumbo and Jumbo.

"Well, pachyderms, are you ready for your long journey?" He laughed loudly and slapped the cage with his bullwhip. He had turned to walk away when he heard a voice.

"The name is Jumbo and . . ."

"Shush," said Mumbo, "don't say a word."

Ramsbottom had turned quickly to see who'd spoken. There were no other men nearby. "How strange," he mumbled, "I could have sworn I heard voices."

Mumbo had her trunk across Jumbo's mouth in case he blurted anything else. Ramsbottom got close to the cage and stared hard at them. "It was hardly these two dumb animals talking." He scratched his head then walked away.

"Phew, that was a near thing," said Mumbo.

"Yes," said Jumbo. Then he began to sing. "Oh, solo mio!"

"Quiet," snapped Mumbo.

"No need to be snappy. I was only going to sing to cheer things up. My pappy used to always say: when you are blue sing something."

"Well, that's all very fine but I don't think we should let on we can sing to this lot," said Mumbo.

Ramsbottom returned and pushed his face up against the bars. He stared at them very suspiciously. They just stared back. Then another man arrived over.

"We're all packed up, boss."

"Good," said Ramsbottom. "Let's get out of here before I go nuts."

"Why is that, boss?" enquired the other man.

"Well, I keep thinking I'm hearing voices, then singing."

"It must be the sun, boss. Maybe you should take a rest."

Ramsbottom felt his forehead. "I do feel rather hot. Perhaps I will lie down."

The cages and crates were carried out of the jungle. The animals watched as some of their relatives hidden among the foliage waved a sad goodbye to them. Soon they were at a busy harbour. Gulls and terns circled overhead. The animals had never seen so many humans before. They seemed to be everywhere. Loading and unloading ships – fishing boats and sailing vessels.

Then one noisy steamboat kept blowing a whistle. "That's the one you beauties are bound for," said Ramsbottom to Mumbo and Jumbo.

Soon they were carried onto the steam boat by several strong men. Some cages were lifted by a crane. Mumbo and Jumbo too were hoisted in the air.

"Aaah," said Jumbo, "I'm getting dizzy – even the birds are lower than us."

"Keep still," said Mumbo. "You're rocking the cage."

Jumbo held onto Mumbo tightly. "If this is what it's like to be a bird, then I'm glad I'm a hippo."

There was a loud thud. Mumbo looked around. She could see the jungle in the distance and when she looked in the other direction there was nothing but blue sea. "Is it safe to open my eyes?" asked Jumbo.

"Yes," said Mumbo. The steamboat sailed out slowly from the harbour. "Take a look at our home," she pointed with her trunk. "It's the last we'll see of it for a very long time – perhaps forever," she sighed.

"Cheer up," said Jumbo. "It's only our home where the beautiful sunbirds sing each morning, and the rainbow gathers by the waterfall and the riverbank where we love to bathe and the waterhole where we all meet in friendship."

The other animals could hear Jumbo. Soon they were sobbing their hearts out. Even Crackle the croc was crying real tears.

Ramsbottom was talking to the captain of the boat when he noticed lots of water near the cargo. "Look," he pointed to the water. "Has your boat sprung a leak?"

"Certainly not," said the captain. They went to investigate the matter.

"Holy smoke," said Ramsbottom, "they're all bawling their eyes out. Quick," he shouted to his assistant, "get some food for them before we are up to our necks in water."

The men hurried back with fresh cabbages, lettuces, carrots, apples, bananas, and meat for the carnivores.

"Something smells good," said Jumbo. The men pushed bags of carrots and fruit into their cage. The sight of food took their minds off their predicament. Jumbo tucked into the carrots. "Very tasty," he remarked.

Mumbo wiped her eyes with her trunk. "Wow, it's true," she exclaimed.

"What, dear?" asked Jumbo.

"Tears taste salty."

"Fascinating," said Jumbo. "Just taste those carrots. They're delicious."

Ramsbottom was walking around the cages listening to the sounds of munching.

"That did the trick," he nudged his assistant. "Let's hope the trip home will go without any more interruptions."

As Ramsbottom passed by the cage of Mumbo and Jumbo, Jumbo pressed himself up against the bars.

"Thank you! That breakfast was splendid."

"Aaah!" shrieked Ramsbottom. "A talking hippo. I must be going nuts."

"Me too," yelled his assistant and they ran back to their cabins.

"Will you keep your big trap shut," snapped Mumbo. "We don't want to get into more trouble than we're already in!"

"You're right," said Jumbo. "My lips are sealed."

Although their journey was slow and seemed endless, Mumbo and Jumbo tried to keep all the wildfolk's spirits up by singing to them. This they could only do when most of the men were asleep. The captain of the steamer enjoyed the singing. He had no idea this sweet music was coming from Mumbo and Jumbo. He assumed it was from some of the men. When he mentioned it to Ramsbottom, he just looked at him and snapped, "Don't mention music to me."

One morning Ramsbottom had a grin from ear to ear.

"You seem very pleased with yourself," remarked his assistant.

"I am very pleased indeed. I've just received a wire from the New York Bronx Zoo and they will take all the animals – lock, stock and barrel."

"Wow, that's great," said the assistant.

"It is. They'll pay top dollars too," said Ramsbottom smugly. "I've told the captain to steer a course for the Big Apple! New York!" The two men did a dance around each other.

"They seem pleased," said Mumbo. "I wonder why?"

Soon the animals were to find out for themselves. After several weeks' travel they were heading up the Hudson River and waving at the Statue of Liberty.

"I have to admit it's rather exciting being in New York," said Jumbo.

"How would you know?" snapped a hyena in a nearby cage. "You've never been here before."

"Well, if you must know, I get a feeling about a place – a gut feeling and it's usually right," Jumbo replied.

"Well, you do have a rather big gut," sniggered another hyena. They laughed loudly. "Listen, buster," said Mumbo, "don't be rude to my dear Jumbo and stop earwigging."

"Who asked you to butt in, Big Ears?" said one hyena.

As quick as a flash Mumbo extended her trunk into their cage and knocked their heads together.

"Ooouch," they yelled.

"I hate resorting to violence but they had it coming."

Jumbo blinked his eyes at Mumbo. "Am

I really your dear?" The boat lurched to a halt. Jumbo crashed into Mumbo 'darling'.

"Some lovebirds," chuckled the hyena.

"I'm warning you," snapped Mumbo.

"Ignore them," said Jumbo. "They haven't a romantic bone in their bodies."

"Look," said Mumbo. "They're unloading the crates already."

"We're next," Jumbo trembled.

Soon all the crates were unloaded from the boat onto a freight train heading for the zoo. They looked out from the train at the tall skyscrapers and the new ones being built. There were people everywhere, moving about.

"They all seem in a big hurry," said Mumbo.

"Sure is busy," said Jumbo.

"And noisy," remarked Mumbo.

Well, it wasn't long before they were being carried into the zoo. Some animals like the lions, cheetahs and leopards were put into larger cages. They watched as the snakes were placed in the reptile house.

"Look, it's Goo Goo," said Mumbo brightly. She hadn't seen the gorilla since the day of the concert. He was being placed in a big cage on his own. "Poor thing, all on his own," sighed Mumbo.

"Let's hope we're not separated," said Jumbo. They needn't have worried for the zoo keeper seemed very kind and put them alongside animals like giraffes, antelopes and zebras in a big green area surrounded by water. Jumbo stretched and yawned, then charged into the water. "Ah bliss," he beamed and sank to the bottom.

After they had stretched and rested their

weary bodies Jumbo remarked, "If you use your imagination this place could be just like home."

"True," said Mumbo. "Except for the poor animals who are all locked up." They watched Ramsbottom come out of an office kissing a big piece of paper. Then he put it carefully into his wallet. As he passed Mumbo and Jumbo he stopped and stared hard at them.

"Well, I'm sure glad to be rid of you lot," he said, pointing a finger at the two of them.

"The feeling is mutual," retorted Jumbo.

"Aaah!" he shrieked, jumped in the air and ran as quickly as he could out of the zoo. "Good riddance," said Mumbo.

An old elephant plodded over to Mumbo and Jumbo and welcomed them on behalf of all the other animals. She introduced herself. "Ethel is the name. I'm the oldest member of the zoo family. So if you want to know anything, ask me. As you know," she winked at Mumbo, "elephants never forget."

"I'm Mumbo and this is Jumbo," said Mumbo.

Ethel looked surprised. "Surely you mean you're Jumbo and the hippo is Mumbo?"

"No," beamed the hippo. "I'm Jumbo."

"How very confusing," said the old elephant. "I hope I don't forget to remember!"

"Can I ask you two questions?" said Jumbo. "What time is dinner and why have you got such small ears?" Mumbo gave him a kick.

"What he means is . . ."

"I know what he means," said Ethel, a little annoyed. "Meals are the same time every day – at four o'clock."

"Good," said Jumbo. "I'm starving."

Ethel flicked back her ears. "My ears are not small. In fact, they are a perfect size for me. But the reason that they are smaller than Jumbo's . . ."

"Mumbo's," said Jumbo.

"Oh yes, Mumbo. Oh dear, how confusing," she sighed.

"You were saying," said Mumbo. "About your ears!"

"Oh yes, I am an Asian elephant, from that ancient land of India where a species like myself is respected, even adored like a god."

"Jumbo didn't mean to offend," said Mumbo. "He's just so curious."

"And hungry," Jumbo added.

After the animals were fed and the visitors had left, the zoo closed for the day. This was the time when the animals felt the zoo belonged to them.

"All clear," said a toucan as he watched the last of the zookeepers leave.

"Good," said Ethel. She made a loud bugle sound with her trunk to get all the animals' attention. The leopards stopped pacing up and down in their cages. The crocodiles awoke from their dozing. The birds settled on their perches. "Salutations, one and all! Today is a very special day for as most of you are aware we have new guests come to stay, admittedly not of their own choice. But since they're here I want everyone to give them a warm welcome." All the animals made various greeting sounds. Mumbo and Jumbo bowed. "I myself am looking forward to getting to know each one of the wildfolk personally and hearing some exciting stories from Africa."

"Perhaps we could do a little recital for you," Jumbo suggested.

"Oh, that would be splendid," said Ethel. "Listen everyone," her voice went higher she was so excited. "My new friends Mumbo and Jumbo have kindly agreed to entertain us. This is Jumbo the elephant."

"No, I'm Mumbo."

"Oh sorry," said Ethel. "This is Mumbo the hippo."

"No, I'm Jumbo," said the hippo.

"Oh dear, I really am becoming forgetful."

"Never mind," said Jumbo. "Why don't you just relax and we'll begin." The hippo cleared his throat. "We would like to sing you something from Verdi's *Aida,*" said Jumbo.

They began. Their beautiful voices filled the zoo and spilled out into the chilly evening air of the city. In one of the high-rise apartments sat Professor Sharp, music professor from the New York Academy, preparing some food for himself. He had opened the window to let out the smoke, as he'd burnt his dinner, when he was stopped in his tracks by the magnificent singing.

"Guiseppe Verdi's *Aida*, my favourite,"

he sighed. He looked out of the window to see where the wonderful singing was coming from. "Ah, *bella, bella*," he shouted out as he heard another aria being sung. This time it was from Ponchielli's *La Gioconda*. Mumbo and Jumbo sang several favourites from different operas. They finished with a duet from Puccini's *Tosca.* All the animals were thrilled by their wonderful singing. They applauded loudly. They then settled down for a good night's sleep, forgetting all about their worries and loneliness.

The professor ran out into the street to see if he could find the source of the splendid singing. He stopped a policeman and asked him if he was singing. The policeman looked around, then said he wasn't but that he was whistling. The professor then asked the man who was selling hot dogs at the street corner. He said he hadn't a note in his head but his brother Louis who lived in Florida was a fine singer. He stopped a couple who were strolling near Central Park and asked if they could sing. They said no but that they could tap dance. They immediately broke into a dance routine, thinking the professor might be a famous theatre producer. After asking several more people the professor finally gave up and went home.

After that, every evening at the same time he could hear the beautiful singing but each time he tried to track down the singers it proved fruitless. He became so obsessed with the mysterious voices that he could hardly sleep at night. Somewhere out there was a new Caruso waiting to be discovered by him.

One morning Professor Sharp was having breakfast in a nearby café when he overheard two men talking, one asking the other if he thought it was possible for animals to sing and talk. "Why not?" replied the other. "I've seen animals on vaudeville stages do amazing things."

Professor Sharp interrupted and, in great excitement, asked the man if he had proof of such a thing. The man, who was none other than Ramsbottom, told the professor his story.

The professor jumped into the air.

"That's it. The zoo. That's where the singing is coming from!" He linked Ramsbottom's arm and hurried him out of the café to talk to him in private. "Do you realise, if this is true – that a hippo and elephant can sing and we've discovered them – we'll be famous!"

Ramsbottom thought about it for a moment then smiled broadly. "We'll make millions."

"Yes," said the professor. They danced around together only stopping when a policeman arrived on the scene. "There is one major problem," said the professor. "How do we get the animals out of the zoo?"

"Leave that to me," said Ramsbottom. "I'll think up some cock-and-bull story about these animals being delivered to the zoo by mistake and I'll refund them some of the money."

The professor shook hands with Ramsbottom. "You're a genius."

The following afternoon before the zoo closed Ramsbottom arrived with a large truck driven by his assistant and managed to convince the zoo-keeper, by waving documents and money in his face, to release Mumbo and Jumbo. The animals had no idea what was happening. But it was easy to lure Jumbo out by showing him all the lovely fruit and vegetables in the truck. Mumbo followed to keep an eye on him.

Soon they were at the professor's house. He sneaked them up the stairs to his apartment.

A neighbour opened a door and shouted up after them, "No need to go up the stairs like a herd of hippos!"

"Sorry," said Mumbo.

When the man saw the elephant and the hippo he fainted.

It was a bit of a tight squeeze getting through the door frame for Mumbo and Jumbo but once inside it was a big room with a tall ceiling. The professor and

Ramsbottom walked about in circles talking to themselves while Mumbo and Jumbo looked on suspiciously.

"So you two really can sing and talk?" said Ramsbottom.

"Of course," said Jumbo. The men could hardly believe their ears.

"See. I wasn't going nuts – I really heard them singing," stammered Ramsbottom.

"Let's not rush things," said the professor, putting on his glasses. "Open your mouths, please."

Mumbo and Jumbo opened wide.

"What do you see?" asked Ramsbottom.

"Nothing," said the professor. "I was just checking they hadn't swallowed a couple of opera singers."

Mumbo tapped him on the shoulder with her trunk. "Listen, buster, we are vegetarians – herbivores. We don't eat people."

"It's truly amazing," remarked the professor. "Of course," he added, "animals can be taught some simple words – take parrots for example."

"We're not parrots," snapped Mumbo.

"We're artists," said Jumbo proudly.

"We were performing in a concert before we were whipped away by you," said Mumbo pointing at Ramsbottom.

"Take it easy," said the professor. "Have a banana." He gave them one each. "I'm going to see how much you two know." He asked them to sing a musical scale.

"We will for another banana," said Jumbo. They sang their scales over four octaves. "That's amazing," said the professor.

"The bananas, please," said Jumbo.

"Where did you learn all this?" asked Ramsbottom.

"That's our little secret," Mumbo smiled.

"Of course, music is more than a few songs and singing scales. It's a lifetime study," said the professor. He picked up a book on music. "For example, take . . ." he rang his finger along some musical terms on the page, "take 'allegro'. Can you tell me its meaning?" He smiled smugly, thinking they wouldn't understand.

"It's Italian," said Jumbo, "for fast and lively music."

"Though not as fast as 'presto'," added Mumbo.

The professor's jaw dropped open.

"Let me try," said Ramsbottom, looking at the music book at the reference section. "What is grand opera?" asked Ramsbottom.

"It's serious opera, unlike an operetta," said Jumbo, smiling at Mumbo. "It's also opera, made popular in the nineteenth century sometime, without talk only singing. I like to think of it as opera on a grand scale." The two men looked at each other.

"I'll try one more," said the professor. "What is an oboe?"

Mumbo looked at him. "A woodwind instrument used in an orchestra, developed in France in the seventeenth century."

The two men began to whisper.

"These two dumb animals aren't so dumb. In fact they're geniuses," the professor declared.

"We've hit a goldmine," said Ramsbottom.

"Now let me handle them," said the professor.

The two men smiled at Mumbo and Jumbo.

"We're impressed," said Ramsbottom.

"Very impressed," added the professor.

"We'd like you to work for us," said Ramsbottom.

"With us," said the professor.

"Doing what?" asked Jumbo.

"Singing, of course," snapped Mumbo.

"Yes, singing," said the professor. "Entertaining millions of people."

"And animals too," added Ramsbottom - in case they objected to singing only to people.

"What about the zoo?" asked Jumbo. "Won't we be missed?"

"No, I've arranged it all," said Ramsbottom, patting him on the head.

"But we were just getting used to the place. We've made new friends," said Jumbo.

"You don't want to return to a cold draughty zoo where there's nothing to do but pace up and down all day!" said Ramsbottom.

"But you put us there," snapped Mumbo.

"Yes," said an embarrassed Ramsbottom, "but that was before I realised how talented you were."

"Well, that's all right then," said Mumbo.

"Then it's settled," said Ramsbottom.

"Remember one thing," said the elephant. "We don't work for peanuts."

"But peanuts are nice," whispered Jumbo in her ear.

"Of course," said the professor. "We shall all benefit as well as bring joy to millions."

"Here, here!" said Ramsbottom, thinking of all the money he hoped to make from the two of them.

The professor didn't waste any time contacting his friends in the music business. Meantime Ramsbottom moved Mumbo and Jumbo to a large house outside New York which included a swimming-pool. This pleased Mumbo and Jumbo very much. Ramsbottom pampered them with the finest food and plenty of time to practise their singing. He even hired a small orchestra to work with them. The musicians were very impressed with their beautiful singing and their great knowledge of music and musical instruments.

Ramsbottom wanted to keep his talented friends a secret until he was ready to launch them on the stage of the Metropolitan Opera House. The professor was working hard on that task. Ramsbottom then decided they ought to learn to walk on two legs rather than on all fours. This proved to be a lot more difficult than he thought. Mumbo got the hang of it quite easily. Jumbo kept falling over and breaking the furniture. Ramsbottom hired a choreographer to teach them how to walk like stars, how to bow to an audience

and even do a dance routine in case they ever needed it.

One evening while Mumbo and Jumbo were resting by the side of the pool, with Ramsbottom and members of the orchestra, the professor pushed open the patio doors and announced loudly, "The stage is set!" They all looked at him. He removed his top hat and gloves. "You audition for the Met tomorrow."

The musicians clapped loudly. Mumbo and Jumbo were delighted. That night poor Jumbo paced up and down, too nervous to sleep. Mumbo spied him from her bedroom window walking around the pool. She went down to see him.

"Are you all right?" she enquired.

"Not really. I can't sleep. I'm too nervous. I've been trying to count gazelles all night but it doesn't work."

"I think you're supposed to count sheep," Mumbo retorted.

"Oh, you're right," said Jumbo. "Silly me." Then he gave a big sigh, closed his eyes and began counting sheep, "One sheep, two sheep, three sheep . . ." He opened his eyes after the seventh sheep. "It's no good. I can't get to sleep."

"Why don't you lie down in the water? The pool is heated."

Jumbo waddled into the water and settled down on the bottom. Mumbo sang him a beautiful lullaby. Soon he was fast asleep and snoring loudly.

Next day they went for the audition at the Opera House. Passers-by were amazed to see a hippo and an elephant entering by the stage door. Mumbo was nervous but didn't

show it. Jumbo seemed very happy. Then he looked out on the stage from the wings and froze on the spot.

"What's up?" asked Mumbo.

"I think I'm having a panic attack," he replied.

"Don't worry," said Mumbo. "Everyone gets butterflies in their stomachs before a performance."

"This is more like a herd of wildebeest," he complained.

"Listen, if we can perform for the king and queen of the jungle, we can perform for a bunch of humans," she reassured him.

The professor introduced them to the committee and a selected audience. They both walked upright onto the stage. Ramsbottom was also in the audience. He was so nervous that he was chewing his hat.

Jumbo smiled sheepishly. "We'd like to begin by singing an aria from Ponchielli's *La Anaconda.*"

Mumbo pushed him. "He means *La Gioconda.*"

"Oops, that's it. Silly me," said Jumbo.

The professor was beginning to panic, for his reputation was on the line having managed to convince the members of the Opera House not only to audition two unknown singers but two pachyderms from Africa.

They sang a number of pieces from Verdi, Bellini, Puccini and Donizetti. When they had finished there was a deadly silence.

"They hate us," sighed Jumbo, "and it's all my fault."

Suddenly there were loud shouts, whistles and handclapping. Ramsbottom looked around to see the expressions on the audience's faces. They were all smiling, some were wiping tears from their eyes and shouting *"Bella!"*

"So beautiful!"

"Wonderful!"

"Sensational!"

"They like us," said Mumbo hugging Jumbo.

The artistic director got up on stage and described them as having voices like angels.

"The new Enrico Caruso and Nellie Melba."

Jumbo gave a sigh of relief.

When they went out into the street, crowds of people had gathered outside the opera house having heard their singing which had carried out onto the streets. The city had come to a standstill. Reporters were there with cameras shouting questions up at them.

"Now that you've successfully auditioned for the great Opera House what are you going to do next?"

"Have a bunch of bananas," said Jumbo. The crowd laughed and cheered. Jumbo looked at Mumbo. "I mean it. I'm starving."

The professor and Ramsbottom were very pleased with themselves. Their next plan was to organise a charity concert in aid of the Children's Hospital and launch their new discoveries at it.

Many big names agreed to take part in the show which was planned for the following month in the Opera House. The concert was a big sell-out. The music critics all agreed Mumbo and Jumbo were the highlights of the show. The crowds loved them and were all looking for autographs as they left the Opera

House. Soon a nationwide tour was organised for the two animal celebrities. It was very exciting for Mumbo and Jumbo to see all the different states. Once again everywhere they

performed their show was an immediate sell-out. Soon they were making a lot of money for Ramsbottom, the professor and themselves. They stayed in the best hotels and ate the finest of foods. Jumbo took to smoking cigars and drinking champagne instead of water. Mumbo didn't approve of this but she too was guilty of overindulging in

large boxes of chocolates and mountains of delicious cream cakes.

One morning Ramsbottom rushed into their home, waving a piece of paper. "Look! We've been invited to tour all the major opera houses in Europe."

"Fantastic," said the professor. "We shall conquer the world with music."

Before they set sail for Europe they received a telegram from the great opera singer Enrico Caruso who wished them every success on their European tour.

"You see," said the professor, "even the genius Caruso recognises your great talent." Things began well for them on their whirlwind tour of Europe starting in the Mariinsky Theatre of Opera and Ballet in St Petersburg, then to Drottningholm Court Theatre in Stockholm. Soon they were performing on the site of the Bastille in Paris where the French organisers promised they would someday build a great opera house.

Then things got a bit dodgy when Jumbo began drinking champagne before the shows. He forgot his lines when singing at the Royal Opera House in London. Then things went from bad to worse when they were booed off the stage at La Scala in Milan because Jumbo had been drinking too much champagne and staggered onto the stage and even fell asleep and began to

snore during the show while Mumbo was doing a solo spot. Worse was to follow when Mumbo, now too fat to get in through the stage door, accidentally knocked down a wall trying to squeeze into the building. Things finally came to a head when Jumbo failed to turn up for the show at the State Opera House in Vienna.

The professor said he was leaving for New York, that he'd had enough of their unprofessional behaviour and animal antics. He had a new discovery that he would manage, a man with a voice like an angel, Beniamino Gigli. He stormed out of the hotel leaving Jumbo lying on the sofa drinking wine and smoking big cigars and Mumbo tucking into Belgian chocolates. Ramsbottom paced up and down scratching his head. He and the professor had made a lot of money out of the talented Mumbo and Jumbo but since they were losing their popularity he decided to sneak off that very night taking all the money including Mumbo and Jumbo's share. Next morning the hotel manager ordered them out of the hotel. Poor Mumbo and Jumbo were now out on the streets with nothing to show for all their concert tours. They sold their clothes for some doughnuts and coffee.

"What will we do?" sighed Mumbo.

"Well, first let's walk on all fours again," said Jumbo. "My back is killing me. I don't suppose we could get back to the zoo in New York?" he wondered. "At least we have friends there and get free food."

"We can't go anywhere until we get some money," said Mumbo. "That guttersnipe Ramsbottom left us in a right pickle."

They walked the streets. No one took much notice of them. "I feel like an invisible elephant," sighed Mumbo, "the way people walk by without so much as a glance. It's not as if we're not big enough."

"That's the problem with people, rushing about all the time just like worker ants back home," said Jumbo. Mumbo's eyes filled with tears at the mention of home. "There, there," said Jumbo. "Remember when you're down, there's only one place to go

and that's up." Suddenly he pricked up his ears. "Listen, I hear music."

They looked around the corner and there was a man winding a strange box and music was coming from it. On top of the box was a dancing monkey, dressed in red.

He was holding a tin cup. "Spare a bit of change?" said the man as people passed by.

"Look," said Mumbo, "people are giving the monkey money. They're buskers! That's what we'll do," she said brightly.

"We'll busk our way back to New York."

"Good idea," said Jumbo. They hurried to a spot near a park where there were a lot of people passing by. Jumbo cleared his throat. "Right, let's begin."

They broke into beautiful singing and people stopped to listen. They sang several songs. People clapped loudly and threw them some coins. "Wow, we've collected enough money to buy some cigars and champagne."

"No more cigars or champagne," snapped Mumbo. "We're only going to use the money for food and for our passage back to New York."

"You're right," said Jumbo,

"And I will give up chocolates," said Mumbo, ". . . for now!"

That night after a good meal they slept in the park. It was cold and rather wet but they didn't mind as they were used to sleeping outdoors back home. Over the next few weeks they performed in different parts of the city and collected enough money to travel first-class back to New York.

"Ah, look at the Statue of Liberty," said Jumbo, looking out the window as they reached their destination.

The first thing they did was to visit the zoo. They could do this only after dark in case the keepers mistook them for escaped animals. Their friends were delighted to see them and they entertained them with an evening concert of their favourite jungle songs. Well, as luck would have it, the professor and Ramsbottom were having dinner in a restaurant nearby when they heard the music.

"Mumbo and Jumbo," yelled the professor.

"Impossible," said Ramsbottom.

They ran out of the restaurant to see where the singing was coming from.

"The zoo!" they shouted together. They ran around the corner and smack into Mumbo and Jumbo.

Mumbo grabbed the two of them with her trunk and raised them in the air.

"Wait, we can explain," yelled Ramsbottom.

"Where's our money?" snapped Jumbo, "Tell us before I sit on the pair of you."

"You mean you didn't give them their share?" said the professor.

"I meant to," said Ramsbottom. "It just kind of slipped my mind."

"Well, it didn't slip my mind! We elephants never forget," retorted Mumbo.

"We can work this out," said the professor in a calm way. "Why don't we all go for dinner?"

"Now you're talking," said Jumbo.

The professor brought them back to the restaurant and ordered the finest dishes for his dear friends Mumbo and Jumbo. After dinner he insisted that Ramsbottom write a cheque for all he owed them. Ramsbottom reluctantly wrote the cheque. Then he handed over the paper.

"There's enough money for you two to buy your entire jungle," said the professor.

"You mean we can buy our own jungle!"

"Yes," said the professor. "It can be your very own nature reserve."

Mumbo and Jumbo looked at each other and smiled broadly.

"Right," said Mumbo, "that's what we'll do. Tomorrow you arrange to buy our jungle, then book a steamship back to our home for us all."

"What do you mean 'us all'?" asked Ramsbottom.

"All the animals in the zoo that want to come."

"But that's impossible," said Ramsbottom.

"Nothing is impossible," said the professor. He whispered in Ramsbottom's ear, "Remember our newest talent is making his debut in the Met next week and we don't want these around interfering or talking to reporters at the *New York Times*."

"No tricks," growled Mumbo.

"No, we were just planning things," smiled the professor.

It took several days for the paperwork to be completed. Ramsbottom bought the land and hired a steamboat for their passage.

That night Mumbo and Jumbo explained what was happening to all the zoo animals. Some decided to stay; others were only too eager to go home.

One night under the cloak of darkness Mumbo and Jumbo knocked down the gates of the zoo and released the animals from their cages. As they headed down the road towards the docks two policemen spotted them.

"What's going on here?" one asked.

Ramsbottom and the professor explained they were part of a circus going to do a show out of town. The police looked suspiciously at them but let them go.

Goo Goo the gorilla gave Jumbo a big hug. "Thanks, buddy."

Doris hugged Mumbo. "Oh, think nothing of it," Mumbo beamed.

They thanked the professor and Ramsbottom and wished them luck with their new singer.

Having said their goodbyes, they sailed at the first light. Ramsbottom had got the same captain who brought them to New York to return them home.

The journey home was very enjoyable with lots to eat and plenty of singing. A swallow had gone ahead to tell the news about their homecoming. When they eventually got to their jungle all the animals were there to greet them including the king, queen and the pride of lions.

There was a great party with lots of celebrations which lasted for days.

"When you two are fully rested we must have a homecoming concert," suggested the king.

"We would be honoured," said Mumbo and Jumbo.

"And I will gladly arrange it," said Doris the ostrich.

"Let's have three cheers for Mumbo and Jumbo," said the queen. The animals cheered loudly.

"It's good to be back home," said Jumbo. "And the first thing I'd like to do is have a good ol' mud bath."

"Me too," laughed Mumbo.

The End